Why do the leaves fall?

T.J. Martin

AuthorHouse™
1663 Liberty Drive, Suite 200
Bloomington, IN 47403
www.authorhouse.com
Phone: 1-800-839-8640

First published by AuthorHouse 9/8/2009

ISBN: 978-1-4389-4329-9 (sc)

Printed in the United States of America
Bloomington, Indiana

This book is printed on acid-free paper.

authorHOUSE®

"Why do the leaves fall?"

The air is cold, the skies are gray, and the leaves are falling.

But why do they fall? Are they tired?
Do they want to be on the ground?

Why do the leaves fall?

Oh look! There's Mr. Squirrel, lets ask him why the leaves fall.

"Mr. Squirrel, why do the leaves fall?"

He is so busy running around gathering nuts and acorns.

"I can't stop and visit with you. I must get these nuts and acorns up to my nest."

We still don't know why the leaves fall this time of year.

Oh look! There's Mrs. Owl.

"Mrs. Owl, why do the leaves fall this time of year?"

"Hoot, Hoot, I'm very tired and must rest in my tree. Good night."

We still don't know why the leaves fall this time of year.

Oh look! There's Mr. Deer.

"Mr. Deer, why do the leaves fall this time of year?"

"I'm not sure why they fall, but they do make a nice bed upon to sleep."

We still don't know why the leaves fall.

Oh look! There's Mrs. Rabbit.

"Mrs. Rabbit, why do the leaves fall this time of year?"

"I can't stop now. Must get down in my hole and sleep."

We still don't know why the leaves fall.

Oh look! There's Mr. Bear.

"Mr. Bear, why do the leaves fall this time of year?"

"Maybe they just like it on the ground."
"Goodnight, I must go to my cave."

We still don't know why leaves fall this time of year.

Maybe we'll never know why.

Just then, Mr. Ranger walks up and asks why we are so sad.

"Mr. Ranger, we have asked Mr. Squirrel, Mrs. Owl, Mr. Deer, Mrs. Rabbit, and Mr. Bear why the leaves fall. They wouldn't tell us. We still don't know."

Mr. Ranger smiles and says, "I do have time to tell you why the leaves fall this time of year."

"Please tell us Mr. Ranger!"

Mr. Ranger says, "The leaves are falling because there is less sunlight. The days seem to be getting shorter during this time of year."

"So the leaves turn pretty colors and fall to the ground."

"The leaves will disappear from the trees in the winter, but they come back in the spring." "Can you guess what color they are in the spring?"

Now we know why the leaves fall to the ground this time of year!

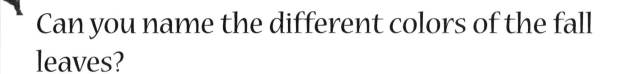

Can you name the different colors of the fall leaves?

How many different colored leaves are there?

What is your favorite fall leaf color?

The End

LaVergne, TN USA
01 October 2009
159582LV00004B